JAMES MADISON

by Candice Ransom

Cody Koala
An Imprint of Pop!
popbooksonline.com

abdopublishing.com
Published by Pop!, a division of ABDO, PO Box 398166, Minneapolis, Minnesota 55439.

Printed in the United States of America, North Mankato, Minnesota

042018
092018

THIS BOOK CONTAINS RECYCLED MATERIALS

Cover Photo: Shutterstock Images
Interior Photos: Shutterstock Images, 1, 16, 19 (top), 19 (bottom left), 19 (bottom right), 21 (top), 21 (bottom left); North Wind Picture Archives, 5, 7, 15 (bottom left), 15 (bottom right); Ian Dagnall/Alamy, 8; iStockphoto, 11; Cory Clark/NurPhoto/Sipa USA/AP Images, 12; Gerry Embleton/North Wind Picture Archives, 15 (top), 21 (bottom right)

Editor: Charly Haley
Series Designer: Laura Mitchell

Library of Congress Control Number: 2017963383

Publisher's Cataloging-in-Publication Data
Names: Ransom, Candice, author.
Title: James Madison / by Candice Ransom.
Description: Minneapolis, Minnesota : Pop!, 2019. | Series: Founding fathers | Includes online resources and index.
Identifiers: ISBN 9781532160219 (lib.bdg.) | ISBN 9781532161339 (ebook) |
Subjects: LCSH: Madison, James, 1751-1836--Juvenile literature. | Founding Fathers of the United States--Juvenile literature. | Statesmen--United States--Biography--Juvenile literature. | United States--Politics and government--1783-1789--Juvenile literature.
Classification: DDC 973.4 [B]--dc23

Hello! My name is

Cody Koala

Pop open this book and you'll find QR codes like this one, loaded with information, so you can learn even more!

Scan this code* and others like it while you read, or visit the website below to make this book pop.

popbooksonline.com/james-madison

*Scanning QR codes requires a web-enabled smart device with a QR code reader app and a camera.

Table of Contents

Chapter 1

Growing Up

James Madison grew up in the **colony** of Virginia. Great Britain owned the American colonies. James was shy and had a soft voice.

James's nickname was Jemmy.

Watch a video here!

Chapter 2

A New Country

The colonies wanted their own country. They fought against Britain in the **American Revolutionary War**.

Learn more here!

Madison

The Americans won. The colonies became the United States of America.

A group of people met to create the US government. Madison took notes. Sometimes he spoke up in his soft voice. The others listened.

The group wrote new laws called the **Constitution**. Madison added special laws called the **Bill of Rights**. They protect Americans' individual freedoms.

One freedom in the Bill of Rights is the right to free speech. This means people can peacefully say what they think. Another is the freedom to have any religion or none.

Public protests today are protected by the Bill of Rights.

Chapter 3

President Madison

Madison became the fourth president of the United States. Then a British ship shot at an American ship. The War of 1812 started.

Complete an activity here!

Madison's home

Madison worked for peace between America and Britain.

Madison was president for eight years. Then he went home to Virginia. He died at age 85.

Madison usually wore black clothes.

Chapter 4

America Today

Madison was a **Founding Father**. He is called the father of the Constitution because he wrote the Bill of Rights.

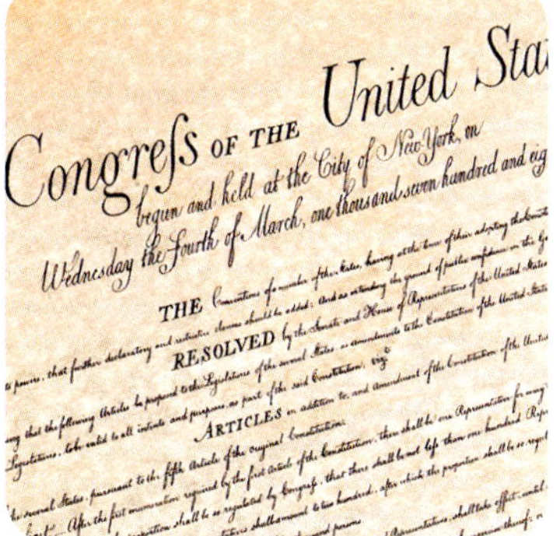
Congress OF THE United Sta
begun and held at the City of New-York, on
Wednesday the Fourth of March, one thousand seven hundred and eig
THE
RESOLVED
ARTICLES

Learn more here!

Today, we still have the freedoms in the Bill of Rights. For example, people who gather to protest are using their right to peacefully assemble.

1751

On March 16, Madison was born in Virginia.

1787–1788

Madison helped create the Constitution. He wrote the Bill of Rights.

Congress of the United S
begun and held at the City of New-York, on
Wednesday the Fourth of March, one thousand seven hundred an
THE
RESOLVED
ARTICLES

1809–1817

Madison served as fourth president of the United States.

1812–1815

Madison guided the United States through the War of 1812.

1836

On June 28, Madison died at his home.

Making Connections

Text-to-Self

This book talks about Madison's early life. How is your life like Madison's? How is it different?

Text-to-Text

Have you read another book about a person from the past? What kinds of facts can you find in books about people?

Text-to-World

Madison was a Founding Father. How did Madison's actions shape the world you live in?

Glossary

American Revolutionary War – the war fought between the colonies and Great Britain.

Bill of Rights – part of the Constitution that lists things that all Americans have the right to do.

colony – a land ruled by another country.

Constitution – a set of rules about what the US government can do.

Founding Father – one of the people who helped create the US government.

Index

Online Resources

popbooksonline.com

Thanks for reading this Cody Koala book!

Scan this code* and others like it in this book, or visit the website below to make this book pop!

popbooksonline.com/james-madison

*Scanning QR codes requires a web-enabled smart device with a QR code reader app and a camera.